Wanda's Words Got Stuck

For the wonderful Lewisham Speech and Language Therapy team
LR
For Jenny (JSN) with lots of love x
PB

Text copyright © 2020 by Lucy Rowland
Illustrations copyright © 2020 by Paula Bowles
Nosy Crow and its logos are trademarks of Nosy Crow Ltd. Used under license.

First US edition 2021
First published by Nosy Crow (UK) 2020

Library of Congress Catalog Card Number pending
ISBN 978-1-5362-1719-3

21 22 23 24 25 26 APS 10 9 8 7 6 5 4 3 2 1

Printed in Humen, Dongguan, China

This book was typeset in Old Claude LP Regular.
The illustrations were created digitally.

Nosy Crow
an imprint of
Candlewick Press
99 Dover Street
Somerville, Massachusetts 02144

www.nosycrow.com
www.candlewick.com

Wanda's Words Got Stuck

Lucy Rowland

illustrated by

Paula Bowles

nosy crow

An imprint of Candlewick Press

Wanda the witch liked tall hats and black cats,
and cauldrons and potions and broomsticks and bats.
She liked to arrive nice and early at school
and read to herself as she sat on her stool.

Dragon Droppings

Frog Spawn

Slime

Sunbeams

Unicorn Kisses

Magic

The classroom was calm with no bustle or din . . .

before the big rush when her classmates came in.
See, there was one thing Wanda worried about . . .

It was talking—she tried
but no words would come out!

It made her feel nervous, so shy and so small.
No, Wanda just didn't like talking at all!

But one day, she thought, *I will try to be brave.*
Then maybe my words will see how to behave.
She walked into school and she puffed out her chest
and planned to say "Here!" just like all of the rest.

First Isobel answered, then Sam and Jake too,
and Wanda was next, but her words stuck like glue.

Then suddenly . . .

there was a knock at the door,
and in came a girl she had not seen before.

Miss Cobweb said, "This is Flo's very first day.
Let's make her feel welcome. Now, what do we say?"

"HELLO!"
shouted everyone
all in a rush,

and Flo felt so shy that she started to blush.

Now, some words are meant well
but come out all wrong.
And some are important
(and ever so long).
Some words can be brave,
even if they're just small.
And sometimes, you find,
you don't need words at all.

So Wanda decided to wait for a while,
then gave a small wave and a very big smile.

She thought, *Maybe Flo's feeling shy just like me.*
Flo waved back at Wanda and seemed to agree.

And Wanda and Flo played together that day.
There wasn't too much that they needed to say!

Flo smiled at her friend, and then Wanda just knew
(though she never quite said it) she'd found a friend too.

The next day, after Spells, Miss Cobweb said, "Class!
This year's MAGIC CONTEST is coming up fast!
You'll each need to do your own animal spell."
Poor Wanda went red and she felt quite unwell.

Magic Contest!

$2 \times$ 🫐 $+$ Unicorn Kisses

$+ 1 =$

Flo squeezed her hand tight. "We can practice," she said.
But Wanda, uncertain, just nodded her head.

They practiced each day after school in the park,
trying spell after spell as it slowly turned dark.

"Just ONE more!" Flo promised.
"Let's give a big shout!"

And Wanda tried hard . . .
but no words would come out.

The night of the contest, the school was so busy,
and Flo was excited, but Wanda felt dizzy.
Miss Cobweb called, "Let's put your skills to the test!
It's time for the spells. Flo and Jake, do your best . . ."

Then Wanda watched closely
and waited her turn.
Her tummy felt funny
and started to churn.

Jake lifted his wand, and a black CAT appeared!
And Flo took a breath as the audience cheered.

She conjured a . . .

DOG!

And the dog chased Jake's cat!

Jake magicked a . . .

LION.

They thought that was that . . .

then Flo started chanting a spell,
"HUBBLE BUBBLE . . ."
She conjured a . . .

DRAGON!

Oh! He looked
like trouble!

Now breathing out fire,
the dragon swooped low
and turned with a . . .

WHOOSH

toward a terrified Flo!

Flo gripped her wand tight, but then—what awful luck—
she couldn't remember her words. She was . . . STUCK!

But then came a **FLASH** and a **BOOM**, **WALLOP, BAM!**

as Wanda the witch shouted . . .

And—*POOF*—then the animals all disappeared!
Flo hugged her best friend as the cloud of smoke cleared.

"Hooray!" the class shouted. Their cheers were so loud
that Wanda just beamed and felt ever so proud.

Now Wanda the witch likes to practice her spells

and giggle with Flo when they don't go too well

and chat with her friends in the lunchroom or hall.
But sometimes . . .

she still doesn't need words at all.